The Math In Me

A Story of Perseverance

Written by Ashley Rougier
Edited by Carla McKenzie

ISBN: 9798756272987

Dedication

This book is dedicated to the woman who believed in every dream I ever had, no matter how big or small...To the woman who would always give her last to ensure I never went without...To the woman who taught me to never give up...To the woman whose love and support I never had to question... To the woman who is the embodiment of unconditional love...
Thank you Mama Dukes!

One day in math class, I looked around and saw that all of my classmates had their wiggling hands raised, just begging and waiting for the teacher to call on them.

The sounds of, "Ohhhh ohhh, I know the answer! Pick me, pick me! Me! Me! Me!" filled the air.

I thought to myself, "Could I be the only one that doesn't know the answer?" My eyes scanned the room looking for just one other person that didn't have their hand up just like me.

Sadly, my hand was the only one not raised.

"Should I raise my hand just to fit in?

What if the teacher chooses me
and I don't have the right answer?"

Instead of raising my hand, I lowered my head letting my tears freely flow from my eyes and bounce off of the math kit on my desk. With every tear that dropped the classroom became more and more quiet.

The room seemed almost still and completely silent. Suddenly, my math kit started to shake. With every shake it got closer and closer to the edge of my desk. It took one last shake before it tipped over the edge of my desk and hit the ground.

I heard a voice say, "Don't cry." Looking around for where the voice came from, my eyes hit the ground and focused on what looked like an animated ruler. I rubbed my eyes to make sure I was seeing clearly. As I opened them, I now saw everything in my math kit standing up and moving around like little cartoon characters!

"My eyes must be playing tricks on me. Did my math kit just come alive?

This can't be.
This ruler can't be talking to me."

"Don't cry, you definitely measure up to all of your classmates," said the ruler.

"You just need to look at things from another angle sometimes," said the protractor.

"At times in math you need
to circle back,
make some markings,
and go for it again," said the compass.

"It's okay to make mistakes and start over," said the eraser.

"Remember to write down what you know and show your step by step thinking," said the pencil.

"Maleaha, are you okay?" I heard a voice say. This time the voice didn't sound like it was coming from the ground. As I turned slowly to my left, I heard the voice speak again.

"Don't give up," my teacher, Ms. Ernestine whispered.

Ms. Ernestine continued to tell me that it's okay if I needed more time to process my thoughts and work out my calculations.

"Learning is all about the journey, the mistakes, the new ideas, and the effort you put in, not just the final answer," Ms. Ernestine comforted.

81 82 83 84
91 92 93 94

" And oh," Ms. Ernestine reminded me, "don't forget to pick up your math kit from the floor."

About the Author

Ashley Rougier has been a NYC public middle school math teacher for over a decade. She has had a passion for math since her early childhood years, which inspired her to subsequently earn a bachelor's degree in Mathematics Education from New York University. Later, she pursued a master's degree in Teaching Literacy B-12 from Touro College, grounding her belief that literacy skills are imperative for a child's success in math. Her inspiration to start writing came from her seeing the need for a book that diffuses the fear of math many youth gain at an early age. Ashley has spent her teaching years cultivating a love for math in her students and hopes that this book encourages readers of all ages to see the life lessons of perseverance and self- motivation.

Made in the USA
Coppell, TX
14 May 2023

16845001R00017